A NOTE TO PARENTS

When your children are ready to "step into reading," giving them the right books is as crucial as giving them the right food to eat. **Step into Reading Books** present exciting stories and information reinforced with lively, colorful illustrations that make learning to read fun, satisfying, and worthwhile. They are priced so that acquiring an entire library of them is affordable. And they are beginning readers with a difference—they're written on five levels.

Early Step into Reading Books are designed for brand-new readers, with large type and only one or two lines of very simple text per page. **Step 1 Books** feature the same easy-to-read type as the Early Step into Reading Books, but with more words per page. **Step 2 Books** are both longer and slightly more difficult, while **Step 3 Books** introduce readers to paragraphs and fully developed plot lines. **Step 4 Books** offer exciting nonfiction for the increasingly independent reader.

The grade levels assigned to the five steps—preschool through kindergarten for the Early Books, preschool through grade 1 for Step 1, grades 1 through 3 for Step 2, grades 2 through 3 for Step 3, and grades 2 through 4 for Step 4—are intended only as guides. Some children move through all five steps very rapidly; others climb the steps over a period of several years. Either way, these books will help your child "step into reading" in style!

Library of Congress Cataloging-in-Publication Data:
Thomas, Jim K., 1970– Luke's fate / by Jim Thomas ; based on the screenplay by George Lucas.
 p. cm. — (Step into reading. Step 3 book)
SUMMARY: Continues the adventures of Luke Skywalker, whose first meeting with the droids and Ben Kenobi leads to the realization of his dreams.
ISBN 0-679-85855-5 (pbk.)
[1. Robots—Fiction. 2. Science Fiction.] I. Lucas, George. II. Title. III. Series.
PZ7.T366956Lu 1996 95-51093

Printed in the United States of America 10 9 8 7 6 5 4 3 2 1

Step into Reading™

C L A S S I C

STAR WARS®

LUKE'S FATE

By Jim Thomas
based on the screenplay by George Lucas
Illustrated by Isidre Mones

A Step 3 Book

Random House 🏠 New York

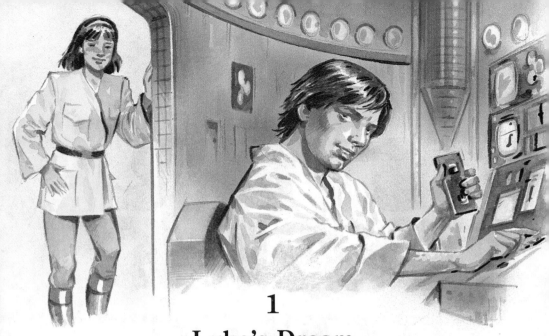

1
Luke's Dream

"Hey, Luke! Where are you?" Windy called.

Luke Skywalker quickly turned off the tape he'd been listening to.

"I'm in here," he called to his best friend.

Windy came through the door of the tech-dome.

"Everybody's going over to Beggar's Canyon to race," she said. "Hey, what are you listening to?"

Windy grabbed the tape.

"'Imperial Space Academy?'" she said.
"When are you going to stop dreaming?
You're stuck here just like the rest of us."

"Whatever," Luke said, grabbing the
tape back. "Let's go to Beggar's Canyon."

Luke and Windy landed at Beggar's Canyon. Their friends were already there.

"Guess what I caught Skywalker doing?" Windy shouted. "Listening to that academy tape again!"

Everybody laughed. Fixer laughed the loudest. He liked to make fun of Luke.

"Hey, Fixer," said Luke. "If you're such a great pilot, how come you haven't threaded the Stone Needle?"

Windy gasped. "That's crazy, Luke! The last kid who tried that almost got killed."

"What do you say, Fixer?" asked Luke.

"I don't need any *shortcuts* to improve my time through the canyon," said Fixer. "But if you've got something to prove, I'm ready to race."

"You're on!" Luke said, heading for his skyhopper. "Come on, Windy. You're riding with me."

The two skyhoppers sped through the canyon.

"This is crazy, Luke!" Windy said. "You can't beat Fixer!"

"We'll see about that," said Luke.

He steered toward a tall spire of rock with a hole in it—the Stone Needle!

"You'll kill us both!" cried Windy.

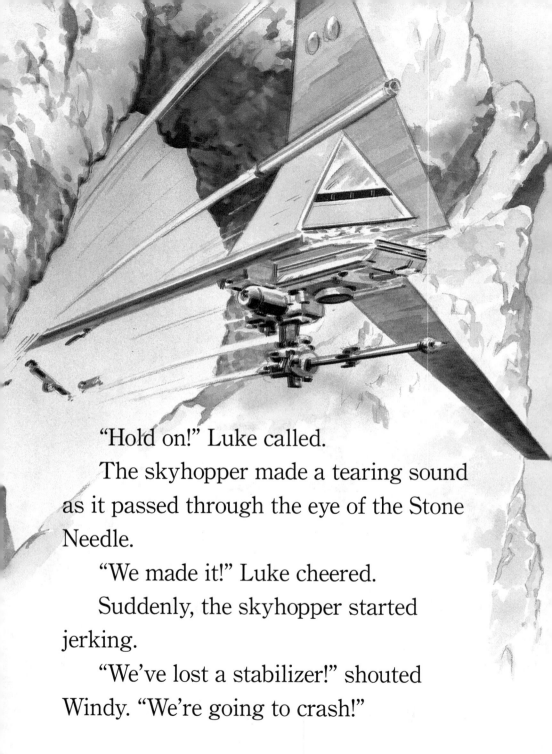

"Hold on!" Luke called.

The skyhopper made a tearing sound as it passed through the eye of the Stone Needle.

"We made it!" Luke cheered.

Suddenly, the skyhopper started jerking.

"We've lost a stabilizer!" shouted Windy. "We're going to crash!"

Luke had to use all his skill to bring the skyhopper to a safe landing.

Windy opened her door. "I'm riding back with one of the others," she said. "You're crazy!"

Luke laughed. He'd done it! He'd threaded the Stone Needle. Now he *knew* he was good enough to get into the academy!

When Luke got home, his Aunt Beru and Uncle Owen were eating dinner.

Luke sat down at the table.

"I'm ready for the academy now, Uncle Owen," Luke said excitedly.

Uncle Owen sighed. "Luke," he said, "you know it's harvest-time. I need you here."

"But you're going to buy new droids from the Jawas," Luke said.

Uncle Owen shook his head. "Droids can't replace you. I'll hire someone to help me next season. Then you can go. I promise."

"That's what you said *last* season," Luke said. He pushed out his chair and stood up.

"Where are you going?" asked his aunt.

Luke looked back at them and said, "Looks like I'm going nowhere."

2
A Secret Message

The next morning, the Jawas arrived in a huge sandcrawler. They brought an odd bunch of droids with them.

Uncle Owen bought two of the droids. One looked like a tall gold man. It knew lots of different languages.

The other was shaped like a barrel. It moved about on three wheels and spoke in whistles and beeps.

Luke led the two droids to the garage.

On the way, the tall gold droid said, "My name is C-3PO, and this is my counterpart, R2-D2."

"Hi," Luke said. "My name is Luke."

"A pleasure to meet you, Master Luke," said C-3PO.

R2-D2 whistled.

Luke laughed. "Just 'Luke' is fine."

In the garage, R2-D2 beeped happily when Luke started to clean him.

"You've been through a lot," he said.

"I should say so, sir," said C-3PO. "What with the Rebellion and all."

Luke turned to C-3PO. "You know about the Rebellion?" he asked.

C-3PO shook his head. "Not really, sir. Only that it's going on."

Luke found a stone stuck between two of R2-D2's metal plates. He used a tool to pull at the stone.

CRACK!

Luke fell over as the stone flew out.

Before Luke's eyes, a hologram of a
young woman appeared. She was the most
beautiful woman Luke had ever seen!

"Help me, Obi-Wan Kenobi," said the woman. "You're my only hope."

Then she said it again. And again. And again. The message was stuck!

Luke stood up. Whoever she was, she was in trouble. And Luke wanted to help!

"Is there more?" he asked R2-D2.

R2-D2 beeped and whistled.

C-3PO turned to Luke. "He says that if you take off the restraining bolt, he can play back the whole message."

"Okay. I guess you're too small to run very far," he said to R2-D2.

But when he took the bolt off, the hologram disappeared!

"Where'd she go?" Luke asked.

R2-D2 beeped and whistled again.

"He says that was a message for Obi-Wan Kenobi," said C-3PO.

"Maybe he means old Ben Kenobi," Luke said.

Luke heard Aunt Beru call, "Breakfast!"

"Keep your eye on R2," he said to C-3PO.

Then he ran up the stairs to eat.

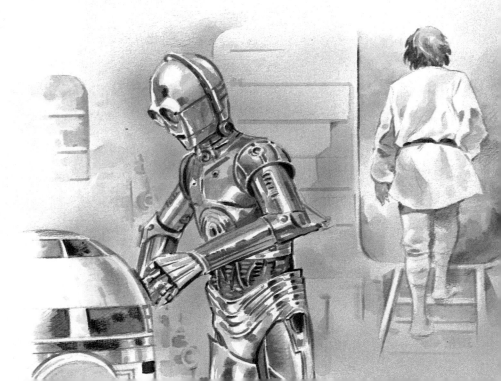

3
Runaway Droid

After breakfast, Luke went back to the garage. The droids were gone!

Luke pressed a button on his belt. If the droids were close by, the restraining bolts would give them a shock.

24

C-3PO jumped up from where he'd been hiding.

"Oh, please don't deactivate me, sir," he said. "I begged him not to go, but he wouldn't listen!"

"R2-D2 has run off?" said Luke.

"Yes, sir," C-3PO answered. "He's gone to find Obi-Wan Kenobi."

"Oh, no!" Luke cried.

Luke and C-3PO rushed outside. Luke scanned the horizon with his macro-binoculars. R2-D2 was nowhere to be seen.

Luke and C-3PO jumped into Luke's landspeeder and took off.

Soon R2-D2 showed up on the landspeeder's scanner.

"There he is," said Luke. "I thought
he might go this way. Ben Kenobi lives
out here. 3PO, punch the overdrive!"

They caught up to R2-D2 in a rocky canyon.

R2-D2 whistled as Luke and C-3PO climbed out of the landspeeder.

"You'll be lucky if Master Luke doesn't melt you down!" C-3PO said to R2-D2.

R2-D2 whistled and beeped.

"R2 says there are creatures coming from the north," C-3PO said.

"Sand People," said Luke. "Let's take a look."

They climbed to the top of the canyon wall. Luke looked through his macro-binoculars.

"That's a bantha, all right," Luke said. "The Sand People ride banthas. But I don't see any Sand People—"

Suddenly, Luke's macros went dark.

Luke looked up to see a Sand Person standing right over him!

With a howl, the creature swung its club.

Then everything went black.

4

Obi-Wan Kenobi

Luke opened his eyes. Old Ben Kenobi was smiling down at him.

"The Sand People!" Luke cried.

"Don't worry," said Ben. "I scared them off."

Luke's head was spinning. He closed his eyes and took a deep breath.

"I was chasing a droid who's looking for Obi-Wan Kenobi," said Luke.

"Obi-Wan," Ben murmured. "I haven't heard that name in a long time—a very long time."

"So you *do* know him," Luke said.

Ben nodded. "Oh, yes, I know him."

"Is he dead?" Luke asked,

"Certainly not," Ben said with a laugh. "Well, not yet, anyway. He's me!"

Luke sat up with a start. The droids were missing!

"Where are the droids?" Luke asked.

Ben pointed. "Behind that rock."

Luke couldn't see the droids.

"C-3PO, R2-D2," Luke called. "Come out here."

The two droids appeared from behind the rock. R2-D2 whistled happily.

Luke looked at the old man. "How did you know where they were?" he asked.

Ben raised an eyebrow but said nothing.

Then they heard a roar.

"Let's go to my home," Ben said. "The Sand People are easily startled. But they'll be back, and in greater numbers."

Inside, Ben handed a short metal tube to Luke.

"This was your father's," said Ben. "He wanted you to have it."

"What is it?" Luke asked.

"It's called a lightsaber," said Ben. "It is the weapon of a Jedi Knight."

Luke turned the lightsaber on.

Luke loved the low humming sound the
lightsaber made as he swung it.

"I didn't know my father was a Jedi,"
said Luke.

Ben sat down and folded his arms.

"I taught your father to use the
lightsaber and the Force," said Ben.

"What's the Force?" Luke asked.

"The Force is an energy field created by all living things," Ben answered. "A Jedi can feel it. That's how I knew where your droids were."

Finally, Luke turned the lightsaber off and hung it on his belt.

"Now, little friend," Ben said, patting R2-D2, "let's see what you have to tell me."

R2-D2 turned on his projector. This time, R2 played the whole message.

"General Kenobi," the woman said. "Years ago you served my father in the Clone Wars. Now he needs your help against the Empire. I have given this droid the secret plans of the Empire's new battle station. Please take them to my father on Alderaan. Help me, Obi-Wan Kenobi. You're my only hope."

Then the woman vanished.

Ben stroked his chin and looked at Luke.

"You must come with me to Alderaan," he said, "if you are to become a Jedi."

Luke was surprised. "But I can't go right now! I told my uncle I'd help him on the farm. For a few more weeks at least."

Ben smiled. "Your uncle will be fine without you. Your destiny lies elsewhere."

Luke thought for a moment. Ben was offering so much…

"I'll go with you," Luke said. "I want to become a Jedi, like my father before me."

Ben put his arm around Luke. "The Force is strong in you, young Luke. I will be honored to be your teacher."

Luke walked outside. He looked up at the sky. Soon it would be filled with stars. And soon he would be out there with them.

Luke smiled. The greatest adventure of his life was about to begin!